ADVENTURES OF FOUR PART-2 FOUR IN THE SEARCH OF LUNERK

ABHYUDAY VIJAYVERGIYA

Contents

Preface

The story of the novel 'Adventures of Four Part-1 Four in the World of Jaffinos' continues itself in this book. The four visit Dema again; accidentally this time as well. But they now believe someone's behind the plot. As the story continues, the four learn more about the culture and traditions on Dema as well as in the Enimix Galaxy. The four start to build faith in the people and with great enthusiasm, they help them once more with a trouble that had befallen there.

CHAPTER ONE

IN THE MAILBOX

The way Arjun and Vicky lied was not as they thought it would be. Unlike their expectations, their mum never ever doubted them for that unrealistic lie and closed that matter from that day itself. .

On a bright Sunday morning, the weather was tranquil unlike the minds of the four. They had the last and the toughest exam on the next day. Then they would be promoted to the next class. .

The doorbell rang suddenly when the Verma family was having breakfast. The children's mum opened the door and found to have a letter in the mailbox, which had been of no use for years. .

It was with no sender's address or name and had 'Arjun Gupta' as the receiver's name. She thought that she had no right to open his letter and so, she handed it to him. .

After breakfast, Arjun went upstairs and opened the letter. What he found inside was shocking. There were the same four tickets he had found in the playground a week ago. He now believed what Mridul said earlier. There is someone who wants them to go to Dema again, perhaps so that they could be killed.

He called Vicky upstairs who was still eating his breakfast. After a while, Vicky finished the breakfast and excitedly rushed upstairs to Arjun. As Arjun saw him rushing, he rushed down and said, "Come here, buddy. We need to go to Mridul and Aanya."

They rushed all the way to Mridul's home and rang the doorbell a few times, gasping heavily. Mridul opened the door and Arjun whispered, "Is your mom home?" Just as Mridul was answering, his mum yelled from the kitchen, "Who's there, Mridul?" Mridul replied, "Arjun and Vicky!"

Then Arjun asked him, "Does she know about our expedition?" Mridul shook his head and replied, "Why are you standing out? Come to my room." The two went to the room, while Mridul called Aanya in.

As the four gathered in, Arjun showed them the tickets he received in the letter with no sender's name and exclaimed, "Mridul was absolutely correct. There is someone who wants us to go to Dema, perhaps so that we could be killed." "But why so?" asked Vicky,

"We haven't done anything to anyone together."

"But I think we should not be worried," sighed Aanya, "We don't have the transporting solution." "But if someone has booked our tickets, then he would make us drink the transporting solution too." said Mridul. "So we need to be careful while eating or drinking anything. It will be like a drop of poison if mixed in our food." replied Arjun.

"I don't know why, guys, I have a strong feeling that it was not the last time we met Ponick." sighed Mridul, disappointed. "Hope for the best." replied Vicky.

The four then started to keep extra caution on whatever they ate until the next day evening, when everything messed up. The four were having a cold drink and burger party at Vicky's house that evening, and the purpose of this was their annual examinations getting over. There was a movie show at 11 o'clock after they would've partied, but who knew, they wouldn't be able to make it that late.

The doorbell rang to have the delivery man, short in height, with a paper bag, that contained a large cold drink bottle and four large sized cheeseburgers. Vicky opened the door and received his order from the delivery man.

While the three were just dancing on the music of Jane Flick, Vicky distributed the cold drink into disposable glasses and handed one to each of them, but they refused. They exclaimed, "We'll drink it later, with the cheeseburger." Then they just danced and danced and danced until they got tired.

Then they sat down to eat. When Aanya noticed a ship printed on the disposable plate, she asked, "Have you ever seen the interior of a ship?"

This was the same moment when the four cheered and gulped a sip of the cold drink. They were vanished into the air. The four thought it was a pure coincidence, but was it really like that?

CHAPTER TWO

IN DEMA AGAIN

According to Mridul, what exactly happened to them was when Aanya asked the question, the four thought of the only ship's interior they travelled in. It was the Enimixian Intergalactic Ship. So, as there was the Transporting Solution in the cold drink and they had thought of the Enimixian Intergalactic Ship while swallowing, they were teleported.

"Don't you think that woman seems to be familiar?" stammered Mridul in fear, pointing to the same receptionist that had been there before.

"Now I can see how irresponsible we can be. We knew someone would do this, but still we let that coincidence happen!" said Vicky.

"But the point we need to think about is who mixed the Transporting Solution in the cold drink. If we find him, we would definitely reach the one who wants us to be in Dema." said Mridul, folding his arms.

"I have an idea!" yelled Aanya, "Arjun, you haven't brought the tickets, have you?" Arjun nodded his head. Aanya then said, "What if we just say them that we don't have the tickets?" Vicky replied, "The ship has taken off. If we say so, they might throw us away into the outer space."

"Wait," interrupted Mridul, "What if we just simply go to Dema and come back again. We have already demolished the Jaff-rule. We wouldn't be harmed." "That's perfect!"

After sometime, when they were in their cabin in the ship, they heard some nuisance outside in the main compartment of the ship. When they went there, they found a crowd gathered and a person who looked like a human was apologizing to someone, who had been shouting at him continuously.

The aggressive man was quite tall. He had worn ragged clothes and his left leg was covered with a black cloth that was wrapped tightly with another white cloth which was twisted up. He had worn a pair of an old-fashioned black sunglasses and a piece of cloth on his face, which covered his nose, ears and mouth. He had an ugly scar on the middle of the forehead, which had been filled with blisters and his scalp was nearly bald. He also held a folded piece of paper in his hand.

When Aanya asked some being standing in the crowd what was happening, it replied, "This aggressive person tripped over this Aungerie, and the paper he is holding was exposed in public. And even though the Aungerie is apologizing, he is shouting at him continuously as if it really meant."

"But who is an Aungerie?" asked Arjun. It replied, "Aungerie is the name of your species. It looks as if your education was disturbed because of the Jaff-rule."

As they heard its words, Vicky figured it out that people which look like humans but are not from Earth are called Aungeries and told it to everybody, making them clearer. And after a while, they all went back to their room.

After an hour, the ship entered into Dema, which appeared too small because of an illusion or what they called it at Dema a Juttin. Dema's colour now changed. From russet, it started to get some yellowish in colour. When they were about to land, they got to know that because of the construction of yellow dome-shaped houses, the Dema's colour had slightly changed.

When they were landed and were headed towards the Richentery Palace for help, they had a great welcome. Four soldiers placed a sofa on the russet sand where the four where standing. They were allowed to sit. After sometime, they were presented by the Dema's classical whistling music by the Chyrins, a species famous for their snout gliding from their chin, often mistaken as females.

As their whistling music changed its tune occasionally, it attracted different animals such as snakes, swans, harmless bees and roosters. That was something wonderful they hadn't seen in their entire life yet.

By that time, a red carpet was already laid upon the ground. Their Prime Head arrived at the setup sitting on the same animal which tried to prevent the four from taking the Ivonick Sword the previous time.

The elections were done after the four demolished the Jaff-rule; and Oilan was elected as their Prime Head. He came to meet the four, who were already familiar with them. When they met, Arjun asked, "How is this animal your domestic one? This prevented us to take the Ivonick Sword."

Oilan replied, "This animal is known as Eudolt. It's domestic to the Prime Head. Jaffinos might've sent it to take the Ivonick Sword from you." "And how did you know that we were coming here?" asked Vicky. Oilan replied, "Since you four have destroyed the Jaff-rule, Dema is getting stronger and stronger. We already got to know because of our Spy Agency that you were in the Enimixian Intergalactic Ship and were to land here in Dema. So, I thought to give a warm welcome to the savior of Dema."

"But where's Ponick right now?" asked Aanya. "He doesn't know you are here." answered Oilan, "But why don't you now come to my palace now. It's all safe."

They all were gathered in a large hall with a stretched table placed at the center in the Richentery Palace. Oilan had ordered a soldier to take Eudolt to the large den where it lives.

When the five were sitting together, the head of Dema's Chemical Science Community, Professor Paront Ingers along with the head of Dema's Defence Community, Ponick Kontle seated themselves to talk about something important. This time, Ponick was also wearing a white shirt and blue pants.

At first, when Vicky noticed him wearing a shirt and pant, he said, "You have got a nice pair of clothes this time." Ponick giggled and replied, "Although Kockies like me can adapt themselves for a large range of temperature, I still like to wear clothes for fashion."

"By the way, we didn't notice the similarity between the clothes on Earth and the clothes on Dema. They are all same." said Aanya, "We never noticed Ingers, Oilan, Moven'C, Mevan and Jaffinos wearing the clothes which are similar to some or another sort of dress on Earth."

"Yeah," replied Ponick, "That's something we could've noticed too. And..."

"That's great," said Arjun, interrupting Ponick, "But I have something more important to say. I don't know who, but there is someone who is trying to bring us here in Dema, perhaps so that we could be killed. So it's our four's humble request to you to book our tickets to Enimixian Intergalactic Ship so that we can go back again to Earth, without giving him or her a chance to harm us in anyway."

"Don't be so formal, Arjun. We are friends." replied Ponick, "And why do you think this?" Mridul told him everything that happened to them in the last two weeks.

"Fine. I'll book the tickets now." replied Ponick, as he made some clicks and swipes on his trency. Trency is usually nailed to the table for safety but it can also be loosen and taken from place to place. The people having a loosed trency are mostly rich or with a high post. For them, convenience is more necessary than safety of the trency as they can afford one even if it is *harmed.*

"Why is it not loading, Ponick?" said Ingers, looking on the non-luminous screen on which Ponick was trying to book the tickets. "I don't know but I am trying my best." "Why don't you book it at the site?" suggested Oilan.

"That's a great idea!" replied Ponick, as he then led the four to the station that was still under construction. He said, "The station where people board and get off the Enimixian Intergalactic Ship is now open for people after the Jaff-rule, but is still not ready to land and take-off the ship and is only providing tickets. The ship has to land in the Jasick Forest."

They then entered into a large, dome-shaped structure through a self-operated door and went to the ticket counter. There, a robot employee said, "When the last time the ship landed here, its basement got damaged because of a clump of very strong trees. That is why the head of the Meurin's Transport Community has now decided that they will not land the ship anywhere except on a proper station certified by them."

"In how many days, the station would be ready to land and take-off the ships?" asked Arjun. "Five; in the worst-case-scenario." replied the employee, closing the window of the counter. "But that would be enough for someone to harm us." yelled Aanya. "And even if

we reach unharmed back to Earth, what we will tell our moms about this?" replied Arjun. The four stood helpless and tensed.

"Can't we use Transporting Solution to get back to Earth." suggested Vicky. "Nope; that is for transportations within a planet." replied Ponick, "Else you could've gone back the previous time, when the Jaff-rule was still there."

Mridul, who had a second plan ready most of the times, said, "Ponick, let's not waste time and go to the Richentery palace as soon as possible. There you give us our pendants so that if in case, we are attacked suddenly, we'll have a backup."

The distance between both the places wasn't enough for them to use the Swan carriage. So, the four rushed to the Richentery Palace. On the way, Ponick said, "I have a good news for you." "Please tell it in the palace, Ponick." interrupted Mridul.

While they were rushing to the palace, they saw a statue that somewhat looked identical to Arjun. Aanya pointed towards the statue and questioned, "Is that a statue of Arjun?" "Yeah; I mean no," replied Ponick, who slipped his tongue, "He's a great warrior. He sacrificed his great life for his purpose to end the Jaff-rule, but couldn't gain success. He was the son of Professor Paront Ingers. After his death, Ingers was broken and from that day onwards, he started to like kids." "That's indeed a new fact," replied she. "And honestly," said Ponick, "He would have been very proud of you all, if he was alive, that you have finished the Jaff-rule."

By the time, they reached the palace and told everything to Oilan and Ingers. Mridul then said to Oilan, "Please keep us protected as much as you can." At this, Oilan replied, "We'll try our best to protect the savior of Dema." "It would be better if we rest in the royal room of guests." suggested Aanya.

"No, you aren't our guests, but our dearest friends. We have personalized a room for you all in the Richentery Palace. Toff will lead you there. He's my friend and a personal assistant." Just then with a perfect timing, Toff entered the room. "Whoa!" he wondered, "I am meeting the saviors of Dema in person!"

Toff was a Kockie and therefore, he had a body identical to that of Ponick. What was different between them were, of course, the facial features.

"Listen Toff," ordered Oilan, "You have to lead them to the sixth room in the left corridor." "That's great!" replied Toff, "Come with me, I'll lead you." When they were in the corridors, Mridul remembered the scene when he had escaped from Jaffinos under the riskiest of situations.

Vicky said, "I am sorry, but I forgot your name." "'It's Toff," replied he, "And I don't need to ask yours. Your names are now a part of general knowledge. They are Arjun, Vicky, Mridul and Aanya. And with the end of our conversation, you've reached your destination."

The four entered the large room and were amazed to see it because its beauty was equivalent to the royal room of guests, in which they had been before. It had four shelves that closed under the floor and opened above. Each shelf belonged to each one of the four. It had loads of Yakuni, and the daily use towel, Kallan and even the Ivonick Sword in the one that belonged to Arjun. But there were no pendants.

Just then, Toff entered and said, "Ponick has resend me to tell you about the good news he was to tell on the way back here. He said that these have emerged from your Ording-pendants. Take these." Toff then handed them four belts. "These are Ording-belts, aren't these?" asked Aanya. At this, Toff nodded.

"But what do you mean they have emerged?" questioned Aanya, again. "Although you are the saviors of Dema," said Toff, "You don't know even the basics of Enimix Galaxy. When someone does something appreciable, his or her Ording-ornament develops more features than the previous one and its core that is secured by a glass cover, changes the ornament into an upgraded one."

"So it doesn't mean its emerging." replied Aanya. Toff said, "It does. You will accept the fact that it is emerging only when you see the process, which I think is very rare." Saying this, Toff left the room. They took the belts and tried them on.

CHAPTER THREE

THE LEGEND OF LUNERK

They then wore on the belts and activated them by a switch on the buckle, except Arjun, whose belt was very much loose. "Guys, what I'm going to do? This belt isn't fitting! It's very loose. You see yourself." said Arjun, in a complaining tone.

Mridul suggested him to go to Ponick and ask. "That's a great idea, indeed!" said Arjun, as he rushed to Ponick. But in the corridors, he lost the way. Luckily, he had found Toff with another Kockie on the way.

"Where are you roaming?" asked Toff. "Oh," sighed Arjun, "It is good I've found you! I nearly lost my way." "But for what are you roaming here?" "I want to meet Ponick. I need to talk about this to him." said Arjun, showing him his Ording-belt, "By the way, who is this Kockie with you?"

"Ah, this," replied Toff, "He's Nodu, a citizen of Dema. He needs employment. Since he has good skills, he is appointed to stand outside the gate of your room. He has been memorized the basic ways in the Richentery Palace. For any help, you can ask him. He'll try to solve or let us inform. But as for now, follow me. I'll help you reach Ponick."

They three went to the four's room in order to show Nodu the room where his duty will be. Then they again went to the Prime Head's Personal Conversation Room, where Ponick, Professor Ingers and the Prime Head were sitting.

Toff knocked and Ponick looked out through the peep hole in the door. As he saw Arjun, he let him in. Arjun went inside and saw the Prime Head with the two main ministers, Ingers and Ponick, sitting.

They were tensed and had rested their heads and chins on the forearm, which was rested by the elbow on the table.

"What's the matter?" asked Arjun, having a seat beside Ponick. "A drop of Lunerk has been found and stolen." said Ingers. Ponick said, "Lunerk is a divine potion which has been divided into three drops. These drops are not a mineral like the NSB or Enzimine, but are a solution like the Venzelo, which is often called as the Transporting Solution.

These drops are the best defensive method. You must be familiar with the fact that swords here grow sharper every moment. If one consumes Lunerk, it can even defense oneself from an attack of the Ivonick Sword manufactured five centuries ago.

This potion was developed by Lox Riff, one of the dearest friend of Sir Erinter Ingers. He knew that Sir Erinter Ingers had made the Ivonick Sword and for the good. But in case it gets to the wrong hand, he thought, then the good must have something to defend it against the evil.

He then worked hard for years and developed this potion. He then divided the Lunerk into three different vials and hid each of them in the Enimix Galaxy at different locations.

He even secured them with Lin bubbles, which are though easy to make but hard to destroy. It can be destroyed by nothing but the Enzimine Potion. And it was just found twice in history.

First, in the Broog planet, which is destroyed at present but its particles still orbit around the Frone, the star around which almost all the planets in the Enimix Galaxy orbit, including Dema.

And second, on the Ivonick Sword. You know it. But if someone drinks two drops of Lunerk, it can be destroyed by the Ivonick Sword. But if he drinks the third drop too, Lunerk's defensive ability reaches the highest and the one who consumes it, becomes invincible, at least for that particular moment."

"So," replied Arjun, "You mean someone is hunting the drops of Lunerk and if he succeeds, he would become invincible." "Yes," said Ponick, "It's the fight between the good and the evil. Will you four help in the mission? A mission that involves the search of Lunerk and the person hunting them down. I promise you won't be harmed in any way. Please Arjun. For Dema, will you?"

Arjun felt pity. And because they had to stay there for days, he said, "Well, we're ready. But the day the station would be constructed and certified, we'll resign from this mission."

"By the way," Arjun continued, "you gave us a good news, but it's quite long for my waist." Arjun showed his Ording-belt to Ponick. "Is it really not of your size?" asked Ponick. Arjun nodded his head. "Then it must go under the Divone Transplantation." said Ingers.

"What is Divone Transplantation?" asked Arjun. "Divone is a living thing that acts as the core of an Ording-ornament. Everything you are able to do

from your Ording-ornaments is because of the Divone inserted in it at the time of manufacture. When you struck the Ivonick Sword on Jaffinos's Head-Gem, you actually killed the Divone in it. Give it to me. I will transplant the Divone in it."

Arjun gave his Ording-belt to Professor Paront Ingers, without any hesitation. Ingers exited the room and went to his newly designed laboratory in Richentery Palace. He gathered his team and began the operation.

"Now if you want me to help you, please call Mridul, Vicky and Aanya here." said Arjun, a little rudely. Ponick sent Toff to call Mridul, Vicky and Aanya from room number six. Toff then told Nodu to send the three friends out. As the three came out, Toff accompanied them to the Prime Head's Personal Conversation Room, where Ponick, Professor Ingers and Arjun were sitting.

The three entered and had a seat. They were then told the problem they were facing and their mission to find Lunerk and the person hunting its drops.

CHAPTER FOUR

THE STOLEN MAP

Mridul thought for a while and asked, "Can you tell us something about the environment when Lox Riff created it. For example, the year it was invented and the Prime Head elected then." "Yes," replied Oilan. "It was the year 3472, when Lox Riff, who was the head of Dema's Chemical Science Community then, invented it.

Since Rynsils, the species to which Moven'C belongs, have a long life span, Moven'C was the Prime Head then and still lives." "Anything else?" said Aanya, trying to make Oilan remember more information. "Yes," exclaimed Oilan, "When I was learning to rule a planet from Moven'C, he told me that Lox Riff was one of his dearest friends."

"I have an idea!" said Arjun, "Ponick said that Lox Riff had made Lunerk for good. So, he must have designed a map or have left us a clue. We can ask Moven'C for this. He might know something about it."

"That's brilliant," yelled Mridul, "We should not waste time and proceed. It would be good if we keep our belts activated." Everyone, ready to head towards Moven'C house, stood up and set the chairs in the table again. "By the way, what happened to your belt, Arjun?" asked Aanya.

Just then, Ingers entered the room with a Linol. He said, "You can control Ords better from a Linol than a belt. And as I have transplanted the Divone in it, its specialty has been changed from Tornado to Fire. But you can still make small tornadoes from it. And when activated, the stick can be sucked in the metal ring and the metal ring can then be worn as a bracelet. Pretty much convenient, isn't it?"

Having activated their Ording-ornaments, they proceeded to the house, where Moven'C resided, along with Professor Ingers and Ponick. On the way to his residence, Arjun asked Ponick, "By the way, Ponick, I often wonder how you knew that I would be able to end the Jaff-rule with the Ivonick Sword?"

Ponick chuckled and replied, "There was a Bryocracy that one would end the Jaff-rule after twelve years of it with the Ivonick Sword. Bryocracy is the outcome of a phenomenon in the nature in which everyone can hear a voice that tells the certain future. It is often heard to correct things in nature which go or might go quite wrong." "That sounds crazy!" replied Aanya, who was walking with them.

As the four entered, they were greeted by Moven'C, who was then feeling a little tired at old age, "What brings all six of you here? And why I was not told about the arrival of Dema's Savior?" "Honestly," replied Ingers, "They came here accidentally and so we too didn't know they were to come, until Oilan's Spy Agency saw it."

Moven'C didn't live in the Richentery Palace, as he was old and then didn't had any post; though his dome-shaped house was not much far. But as he had served the post of Prime Head of Dema, he didn't had to earn for livelihood. Instead, his needs were fulfilled by the government.

Rynsils, the species to which Moven'C belongs, was a rather strange species. They had their two nostrils fused in one. And the other features were almost same as those of an Aungerie.

"Why don't you sit and have a cup of Feren tea?" said Moven'C, as he went inside the kitchen. In order

to make Feren tea, he first peeled up the skin of the Feren fruit which was cultivated through Yakuni in Dema itself. Then he ignited a pair of Fibon and kept it in the stove on a stove like structure.

Fibon is a common, reusable, cuboidal-shaped rock found in Dema. It is used to ignite fire there as it is rubbed with one another. It's a completely non-exhaustible energy resource.

He ignited the rock and on a russet-coloured clay pot, boiled the pulp of sliced Feren fruit in Yakuni, after keeping the clay pot on the stove.

Gradually, Yakuni turned into a milk-like liquid and the pulp was dissolved completely in it. He then transferred it into six glasses and served them on a tray to his visitors. "You can now have these glasses of Feren tea." replied Moven'C.

The four didn't like the Feren tea if they compared it to Ponick's, though in their opinion, it still tasted good.

"The first drop of Lunerk has been found and stolen from the Metron planet." said Ingers. Hearing this, Moven'C was shocked and asked in panic, "By whom?" "He's unknown." replied Ingers, "Mridul told me to ask you about Lunerk, when Oilan told him that Lox Riff, the inventor of Lunerk, was a good friend of

yours. Perhaps you might have a clue." "I do." replied Moven'C, trusting them.

"Wait," interrupted Aanya, "Don't you think the word 'Metron' sounds somewhat familiar? I guess we have heard the name before." "Ponick and Ingers have." replied Moven'C, "But I can't say if any one of you four has ever heard of it. Anyways, let me tell you where you would find the map."

Moven'C continued, "There is a red button on the back side of the throne. If you keep it pressed for two seconds, a treasure chest will appear on the seat. Unlatch it manually and you will find the map inside, which will lead you to the other drops of Lunerk."

"Thank you!" said Mridul. Mridul and Arjun were the two who looked the most enthusiastic for this mission than any Earthly creature.

As the visitors were leaving, Moven'C said, "Listen. Test the Ivonick Sword as well. It might not be the real one. Enzimine potion is rare to be found. He might have stolen the Ivonick Sword as well in order to destroy the Lin bubbles with its blade that has the Enzimine potion on it."

That's a great advice, indeed!" replied Ponick, closing the door behind him.

The six again went to the Richentery Palace. On the way, Aanya, who was still trying to remember where she had heard the name before, said "I'm pretty sure that I've heard the name 'Metron' before Ingers spoke of it there. But I am not sure where I've." "It would be better if you yourself think upon it." replied Vicky, "I don't think that anyone of us has heard of it before, except Ingers and Ponick."

They entered into the Richentery Palace and went to the Prime Head's Personal Conversation Room, where Oilan was eagerly waiting for them. Ingers told him everything that Moven'C and they talked about. They deactivated their Ording-ornaments and kept it on the table.

Just after that, they were headed towards the throne in the Main Court of the Richentery Palace, where Jaffinos used to sit from past twelve years and then Oilan, when he had to talk with his ministers, who were actually the head of Dema's various communities.

Oilan went forward and pulled the throne a little forward with help. On the bottom of the back surface of the throne was a red button, as described by Moven'C. Oilan pressed the button for a few seconds and gradually the switch turned green. Consequently, a neat crack appeared on the seat of the throne.

The partition on the either side of the crack functioned as the two panels of a box, which opened. Out of the deep, a chest came out floating in the air. Oilan unlatched the attractive chest to open it. Everyone was getting more curious and had already set their eyes on the chest without blinking. Oilan opened the chest and found nothing inside.

"It's pretty rare to find Lunerk without wasting any efforts for the map. The hunter of the Lunerk must have stolen the map before." yelled Vicky. "I smell trouble." replied Mridul.

Oilan closed the chest and latched it before pushing it deep into the throne and closing the lid on the seat. And then the crack on the seat disappeared and the switch turned red once again.

"I remembered!" yelled Aanya, in a tone of extreme satisfaction. "This time the receptionist said that the Enimixian IG Ship would fly from Metron to Friniwock, with Earth and Dema being its stops in between. That's where I heard the word 'Metron' before Moven'C mentioned it to us."

"Good God!" sighed Arjun, as if he realized something, "The second drop of Lunerk is in Friniwock and we four have seen the person who is hunting them! Do you remember the aggressive person that created commotion on the Enimixian IG Ship? He is the one who has stolen the first drop of

Lunerk and is hunting down the rest."

When Ponick, Ingers and Oilan looked confused, Aanya told them about the incident on the ship where a being of unknown species tripped over an Aungerie and started shouting at him continuously even though the Aungerie was apologizing for his mistake.

Arjun continued, "He got so angry and aggressive not because he tripped over and fell down, but because his folded piece of paper fell down and was exposed in public, which was actually the map that led him to the first drop of Lunerk and can lead him to the rest two drops. That was the map we're missing here in the secret chest.

And because that ship was going from Metron to Friniwock, he must've gone to Friniwock in search of the second drop of Lunerk. Although the Enimixian IG Ship landed on Earth and Dema as well, I guess none of the passengers left the ship on Earth and only a few left the ship on Dema. And I don't think that hunter with weird clothes came down from the ship here."

"By the way, don't you think it's taking too long for us to refer to the person who is hunting the three drops of Lunerk?" interrupted Aanya, "Shall we call it with another name, perhaps easier? Like hunter; Lunerk Hunter; thief; Lunerk thief- or something else if you want."

"Lunerk Hunter!" replied Ponick, "That name suits." "And also a name of our mission?" suggested Aanya, "It would keep us more organized, don't you think?" "Nope," replied Mridul, crossly, "It's not a necessity."

"So, I guess we should leave to Friniwock." said Ingers. "But Moven'C told us to verify the Ivonick Sword too." interrupted Aanya, "How will we do that?" "We'll try to break it." suggested Vicky, "If it breaks, it's fake. That's what poor Jaffinos did. Pity on him."

"That isn't a great idea." replied Ponick, "Some swords other than the Ivonick Sword are unbreakable too. We would have to fly to the clump of Synock Trees, which are unique trees in Meurin that can withstand even a strike of a sword that has an age of forty years. And no sword is more than eighteen years old.

But the Ivonick Sword is an exception with an age of fifty-six." "Don't those trees grow stronger with their age?" questioned Aanya. "Don't be so silly, dear," replied Ponick, "They are not swords."

"If we have to go to Friniwock as well as Meurin, we should go simultaneously." said Mridul, "Professor Ingers, Vicky and Aanya would fly to the clump of Synock Trees in Meurin and I, Ponick and Arjun would fly to Friniwock."

"But how'll we go there?" worried Aanya, "The Enimixian Intergalactic Ship has refused to land here on Dema." "That's a problem." replied Ponick, "Let me think about it." "Swan Carriage would do, perhaps." suggested Aanya.

"No," replied Oilan, "That's only for transportations within a planet. Even though Meurin is comparatively the nearest planet to Dema, you can't go on a Swan Carriage. The reason for this is that the Swan Carriage, which is actually the brand name of a company of Meurin, has built control centers in various planets in Enimix Galaxy and in the basement of each control centers, the carriages pulled by swans are kept, which provide service to that particular planet."

"I have an alternative in my mind." said Vicky. "Speak it up!" replied Ingers. "It's Eudolt." said Vicky, "But it's kind of violent, I guess." "That's a great idea,

indeed!" replied Ponick, "And it's not that violent too. But it can transport just one team. It's not that huge."

"Why not chance-wise?" replied Ingers, "If Oilan could give us the permission, Bono would fly Eudolt to Meurin carrying Aanya, Vicky and me. Then he would bring Eudolt back here and then would carry Arjun, Mridul and Ponick to Friniwock, after which he would simply bring Eudolt back here, riding on it." "It's quite a good idea, and so I allow you to proceed." replied Oilan.

"By the way, who's Bono?" questioned Aanya. "He's my worker who is trained to domesticate Eudolt." replied Oilan, "I would've to admit, he knows his work pretty well. He's actually a Rynsil and has served Eudolt for past fifty years. "

"We should proceed now!" said Vicky, preparing himself mentally for the mission.

CHAPTER FIVE

A VISIT TO MEURIN

Oilan ordered his servant to go to Bono and tell him to bring Eudolt in the front of the gate of the palace. In the meantime, Arjun, Vicky, Aanya, Ponick and Ingers went to the front gate to go ahead with their mission to stop the Lunerk Hunter to succeed.

Oilan came along to tell Bono his work and to give best wishes to the saviors of Dema and the ministers for their mission.

"Bono, drop Vicky, Aanya and Ingers to Meurin, on Eudolt." ordered Oilan, "Also, give them a mini trency, so that they can let us know when to pick them up." Bono used to keep some mini-trencies that were unused. These gadgets can help message to any other mini-trency or a normal trency.

"Sure, sir," replied Bono, "I shall quickly bring one to them." "No, they would be late if you go all the way back to bring just a mini-trency from your Glustra. Go

on Eudolt with Aanya, Mridul and Ingers and pick up one."

"What's a Glustra?" asked Aanya, curiously. "It's a wooden container used to store your clothes, Ording-ornaments, trency, Kallan and more." replied Ponick, "I guess you know them. Those shelves that appear when you pull one of the handles attached to the floor."

"Very well, sir," said Bono, "I shall take an unused mini-trency from my home and then drop them to Meurin."

From inside the palace, came Mridul rushing towards the gate, with the Ivonick Sword and Linol in his hand and something was stuffed inside his pocket. "Hey!" gasped Mridul, as he braked down, "You forgot your Ording-ornaments as well as the Ivonick Sword.

I had to go to Oilan's Personal Conversation Room and then to ours in order to get them. How irresponsible you can be!" Mridul handed the Linol to Arjun and the Ivonick Sword to Professor Ingers. Then he distributed the Ording-ornaments, including Ponick's and Ingers's, to them.

Without wasting another moment, Bono, along with Professor Ingers, Aanya and Vicky, rode to his home to get a mini trency. As Eudolt sat on his hind limbs,

Bono quickly descended Eudolt and went inside and brought with him a mini-trency. He mounted Eudolt quickly and flew off the planet.

Through the calm sky, Eudolt flew up, crossing the atmosphere. Ingers was sitting behind Bono, who was riding Eudolt. Behind Ingers, it was Aanya and Vicky sitting, respectively.

On the way, Aanya questioned, "Why aren't we feeling lack of oxygen here?" Vicky continued, "And on the Enimixian IG Ship as well. Why so?"

Ingers answered, "The Ording-suits, which are activated with the activation of the Ording ornaments, provides the owner with oxygen whenever needed. And as of the Enimixian IG Ship, there is enough oxygen on the vessel to let the passengers survive."

"But Ingers," asked Aanya, "We haven't activated our Ording-ornaments yet." "Really!" cried Ingers, "Are you crazy? I told you to activate them. Activate them this instant or you'll faint and fall off as we'll go up in the atmosphere with decreasing oxygen levels."

Aanya and Vicky activated their Ording-belts quickly, before any accident could take place.

Eudolt braced itself and rode from Dema to Meurin all the way through space. On the outskirts of the civilization on Meurin, Eudolt landed and sat on his hind limbs. Professor Ingers, Mridul and Aanya descended the animal and Bono drove Eudolt back to Dema.

The three walked up a mile to reach the main civilization. They were thrilled to look at the fine architecture of the buildings that were pyramid shaped with a square base.

"It would be better if you two deactivate your Ording-ornaments." said Ingers, deactivating his Ording-pendant, "Roaming in the city with Ording-suits on, could prove to be risky. The local police might investigate us." Aanya and Vicky obediently followed his precaution and deactivated their Ording-belts.

With a much similar climate to Dema, Meurin was considered to be the most industrialized and civilized planet in the Enimixian Galaxy. Meurin had colourful houses, buildings and as well as schools. But the finest of all was the Aschderine Palace, which was the residency of the Prime Head of Meurin, Dareo Ingos, who was an Aungerie. The planet had a vast variety of species, including Kockies, Chyrins, Aungeries, Rynsils, Snakes, Bears, Swans, Bees and more.

Exploring the beautiful planet, Professor Ingers, Mridul and Aanya came across a Jave, which is a species of a rodent like structure with a similar colour and size, which could stand on two legs and had quills on the back like a porcupine. They usually didn't prefer clothes.

Ingers asked him, "Hey, you Jave, listen. Could you please tell us the way to Synock trees?" That Jave had plugged in the same furry balls in his ears that Ponick wore when the last time the four visited Dema and Ponick wanted to maintain his streak.

He ignored Ingers and moved on. Ingers then asked a Kockie and a Chyrin. But they too just ignored him, perhaps considering the then standard of the planet they were from; semi-constructed houses, no schools and no proper port for the Enimixian Intergalactic Ship to land.

Frustrated, Ingers went an exotic cafeteria to have a cup of Feren tea. Ingers grabbed out the mini-trency from the pocket of his pants, just after which, the three had a seat.

"I still have some Enimon balance in this. Tell me what would you prefer- Simple Feren Tea, Diluted Feren Tea, Cold Feren Tea, Feren Fruit Shake?" "The simple one." replied Aanya. "Feren Fruit Shake." replied Mridul, "I guess it would be better."

Ingers called a waiter, who was a Kockie, and told him their preferences. The waiter went back to the kitchen to have their order placed.

"I wonder what Enimon balance is." asked Aanya. "Enimon stands for Enimixian Money." explained Ingers, "It's a type of currency that is run across the Enimix Galaxy. It can be used to purchase anything in the Enimix Galaxy. On a certain planet, it can be converted to the native currency of the planet, which of Meurin is Pums."

After a while, the waiter came back with the Feren Fruit Shake, the Feren Tea and the Diluted Feren Tea, which Ingers had ordered. Seeing an opportunity, Ingers asked him, "Excuse me. Do you know where the clump of famous Synock Trees is?"

The Kockie ignored him and went back to work. "Why the people are not listening to a helpless pedestrian?" yelled Ingers, "I am frustrated! Even though the Synock Trees are worshipped, still none listens to me. Is there something that I don't know?"

CHAPTER SIX

TO FRINIWOCK

As Arjun, Mridul, Ponick and Oilan stood waiting outside the Richentery Palace in Dema, Eudolt landed in front of them, with Bono sitting on it, holding its rein.

Eudolt sat on its only pair of limbs, so that Arjun, Mridul and Ponick could ascend it. As the four creatures settled upon the scaly skin of the animal, it flew up through the atmosphere. Oilan, who remained there only, waved at them and wished, "Good Luck!"

As Eudolt was flying up, Ponick told them, "Activate your suits. They will provide you with oxygen in the space." Mridul activated his Ording-belt whereas Arjun activated his Ording-Linol, which looked pretty cool.

That structure of a rod and a metal ring upon it had another feature. The rod could be sucked in by the metal ring and the ring was large enough to be worn as a bracelet; and still the Linol could be activated as an Ording-ornament.

Mridul's suit as well as Arjun's was now blue and white in colour, because the Divone, the core, in it had been upgraded to belt level. As Eudolt was flying up in the space, Ponick told them, "Friniwock is actually friendly to Dema. So it's easy to find the 'Lunerk Hunter'."

It was just an hour that Eudolt took to reach Friniwock. Eudolt didn't land in a remote area on Friniwock like on Meurin, instead it landed on the expansive royal fields beside the Prime Head's residency, the Krate Palace. Arjun, Mridul and Ponick descended from Eudolt and Bono drove Eudolt back to Dema.

Suddenly, an army of soldiers appeared before them, which made Arjun and Mridul think that they were in trouble. Then unexpectedly, the soldiers divided into two groups- one that stood on the left and the one on the right. And from between, came Tivit Symick, the Prime Head of Friniwock.

Tivit Symick was a Shronne, which was a species similar to Rynsils, the species with fused nostrils. A major feature that differentiated Shronnes from Rynsils was that the Shronnes had a pair of small horns in their head, whereas Rynsils didn't. And to hide those horns, most Shronnes kept long hairs, like

Oilan Syman and Tivit Symick, the Prime Heads of Dema and Friniwock respectively.

"Welcome, Ponick," greeted Tivit, "It's such a pleasure to meet you." "It's nice to meet you as well, Tivit." replied Ponick. "You are Arjun and you are Mridul." guessed Tivit, at which they both nodded, "Oilan told me about your arrival through the Intergalactic trency. He told me you are looking for someone whom you suppose is in Friniwock."

"Yes," replied Ponick. "Then why're you waiting here outside? Let's come in, Ponick, Arjun and Mridul."

Tivit, Ponick, Arjun and Mridul went to the Main Court inside the Krate Palace, and the army to their base. The palace was an ordinary one, but was built at an altitude.

"So now tell me whom are you searching for?" asked Tivit. "You know about Lunerk, don't you?" said Ponick. "Yeah I do know about it very well." replied Tivit. Ponick exclaimed, "Its first drop has been stolen and the second drop must be in Friniwock." "And why do you think so?" asked Tivit.

At this, Ponick told him everything that had happened in the Enimixian IG Ship, when the four were travelling from Earth to Dema, and the logic with which they suppose that Lunerk Hunter must be in

Friniwock, in the search of Lunerk.

"Very well," replied Tivit, "But what do you want me to do for you?" Ponick replied, "Lunerk is important and it should not be in the wrong hand. If it is, then the whole galaxy would be in grave danger. I know it's expensive, but in my opinion, you should send an army in the remote areas of Friniwock and make the population aware of it as well as keep a reward for whoever finds the 'Lunerk Hunter'. And don't forget to keep a check on the passengers that travel through the Enimixian IG Ship, from which the 'Lunerk Hunter' may try to escape."

"That's a great idea, no doubt," replied Tivit, "And you should not worry for the expenses as well. But how the people or the army would know how the 'Lunerk Hunter' looks?"

"I know how he looks." exclaimed Arjun suddenly, "He has very distinct facial features and a dressing sense that would significantly help us to recognize him. He is quite tall, but bald. He wears ragged clothes and his left leg is abundantly tied with cloth. He had a pair of black sunglasses on and a masked face. There was also a scar on his forehead and he may have a folded piece of paper in his hand, which is none other than the stolen map."

"That's great," replied Tivit, "Don't worry now; I'll take all the necessary steps. For now, you must go

to the Royal Room for Guests and take an afternoon nap."

Ponick, Arjun and Mridul went to the Royal room for Guests in the Krate Palace, accompanied by a servant, who was a Jave. Mridul, who was feeling a little shy in front of Tivit, asked Ponick, "Ponick, shouldn't it be night by now?" "It is," replied Ponick, "but in Dema. Don't forget we're in Friniwock; time here is slightly different."

The room was awesome, but not much like the one in the Richentery Palace in Dema. The three slept peacefully for a period of time. After they had a power nap, they were provided with Kallan, to wipe their face with.

Kallan is a daily-use towel that makes one fresh when wiped up the face with, usually on morning or after naps.

As Ponick, Mridul and Arjun woke up, they were called to the Control Room of the Krate Palace. There were thousands of buzzers, buttons, levers, switches, indicators, lights and fourteen screens. And no doubt, that it was a huge one.

Arjun and Mridul were asked to sit and examine the camera footage, because they had seen the 'Lunerk Hunter'. The camera was fitted on the helmets of the chiefs of different army units that was sent to remote areas of the planet.

Overtime, the news about the reward was spread to such an extent, that people were sending fake photographs to the given trency address. Out of thousands of photographs from around the planet, only one or none might've been the culprit.

Arjun was asked to stand up and sit on another chair so he could check the photographs sent by the public. Gradually, Arjun checked all the photographs thoroughly and Mridul too examined the video footage, but no 'Lunerk Hunter' was seen.

Tivit and Ponick were sitting on the other corner of the room, discussing what other steps shall be taken, when there was a knock on the door. Tivit unlatched and opened the door and a soldier, who appeared before him, said, "There's a saint at the entrance of the palace who wishes to meet you. He is saying that he knows where the second drop of Lunerk in Friniwock, lies."

CHAPTER SEVEN

THE SYNOCK TREES

Ingers was irritated when none was paying attention to him in Meurin. He thought for a while, until he drank his Diluted Feren Tea and cried, "I got it! I know why none listens to me."

He stood up and went to the counter. He paid the bill in enimons and said, "Ai- go- li- wo- Synock- vell- gob-" In a similar tone, the cashier replied back, "Ity- ouve- wo- ine- gree- inet- Campute Krail- inet- wolly me- Gojavu Breem."

Ingers, with extreme satisfaction, rushed out of the cafeteria, where Aanya and Vicky followed him after having their drinks, confused. Outside, Aanya asked him, "Hey professor! What happened and why were you and the cashier making such strange noises?"

"I forgot that the people of Meurin speak Nenilan, which is the Enimixian Galaxy's native language. And because of their busy schedule, they ignore if people

or other creatures utter uselessly. I asked him about the Synock trees and he told me where they are- in the Gojavu region of the Campute state."

"But Ingers, why do we speak English in Dema?" asked Aanya, "I mean how you people know English?"

"That's a history. We, people in Dema, know Nenilan and English both. But I'll tell you that later. For now, we need to book a Swan Carriage to go to the Gojavu region of the Campute State."

Ingers, who had held the mini-trency in his hand, ordered a Swan Carriage of Meurin so as to reach the clump of holy Synock Trees.

Shortly after, as the Swan Carriage landed outside the cafeteria in Meurin, Professor Ingers, Aanya and Vicky ascended it and said the name of their destination, "Gojavu region of the Campute state."

Since Ingers wanted to travel few times in Meurin, he did not take the subscription like in Dema, instead he paid for every ride he took through the mini-trency using enimons.

There were at least a dozen more Swan Carriages flying, that Vicky and Aanya noticed on their way to Synock Trees. For Ingers, it wasn't a new thing since he had visited Meurin several times before the beginning of Jaff-rule.

Soon, they descended the Swan Carriage as it landed on its destination. Ingers went forward and asked a pedestrian in Nenilan, "Ai- go- li- wo- Synock- vell- gob-"

"Cotte pil- reg- doom- we- cojito- mi- vugo- jani-" replied she, in the same language, Nenilan.

Ingers rushed when he got to know the exact address of Synock trees, with Aanya and Vicky following him behind. They stood on the queue that included the public who wished to see and worship the Synock Trees. Shortly after, their turn came.

There was a railing in front of them and on the other side of it stood some guards, ensuring none shall trespass. Ingers was shocked to see the guards there as he never expected the presence of security. He said something in Nenilan to the guard and the guard replied back in a similar tone. A long conversation followed in Nenilan.

Ingers, who was extremely disappointed, went out of the queue and sat on a bench beside. "Professor Ingers," said Vicky, "What did you talk there and what happened?"

Ingers replied, "The guard said that observing the decreasing population of the Synock Trees, the government has imposed a ban on the cutting of them. The trees will now always be protected by the government. I even told him that we have an urgency and it's a crisis with which the whole galaxy can be suffering in the future. But he wouldn't listen."

"So what shall we do now, professor?" asked Vicky. "What about an underground tunnel?" suggested Aanya. "Are you crazy?" yelled Vicky, "What if we get caught? Didn't you realize how strong the guards were?" "Why don't we call Oilan on the mini-trency and tell him what has happened?" asked Aanya.

"No, calls on mini-trencies are not for intergalactic purposes. But you're right. We can at least text him. We should call Bono here on Eudolt so that he could pick us up."

Saying so, Ingers grabbed the mini-trency from his pocket and texted Oilan,

"Oilan, we are unsuccessful. Please send Bono here with Eudolt as quick as possible. We need to use this sword only. What we can do is nothing but just hope this is the real Ivonick Sword."

CHAPTER EIGHT

A CUP OF FEREN TEA

It was night in Dema. As Oilan was going inside the Richentery Palace, he felt like he was forgetting something important. He tried to remember what he had forgotten.

After thinking for a while, when he couldn't remember anything, he gave up and decided to ignore it. He went in his room in the Richentery Palace and decided to sleep. But the feeling was so strong that he couldn't just simply ignore it. So he decided to have a cup of Feren Tea.

Oilan was the Prime Head of Dema and resided in the Richentery Palace, so he could obviously ask the Royal Chef to serve him one cup even in the night, but he didn't.

It was not because he was generous and didn't want the chef to be disturbed, but because he didn't like the Feren Tea made by him. He always requested Ponick to make some Feren tea for him as well, and indeed, Ponick used to make some for him. But since Ponick wasn't there then, he decided to make some himself.

He went to the library in the Richentery Palace and searched for a book on cooking. Soon, he found one and went to the kitchen with it. Following the instructions carefully, that were written on it in Nenilan, Oilan made a perfect tea for himself.

He tasted it and realized the presence of a wonderful skill in him. He then sat on a chair in the balcony, facing the lake that showed the reflection of the moon beside the palace. He then tried to remember what he had forgotten. All of a sudden, he realized and went to his trency to call Bono.

Bono was in his home, playing Danglo and Nutt, waiting for the text message that shall tell him to go on the other planets with Eudolt and pick six of them up.

Danglo and Nutt was a musical instrument in Enimix Galaxy, in which a string with varying thickness called Danglo was tied on a vertical piece of wood and was struck with a finger-like structure called Nut, to produce sound. Different notes could be played by striking the Danglo with the Nutt on different points.

His trency was kept on a table beside, when Oilan called him and it rang. Bono went to the table and accepted the call.

"Bono," said Oilan, "Did you give a mini-trency to Ponick as well?" "No, master," replied Bono, "I didn't." "Then how will they text us when their mission will get over? Leave everything you're doing right now and go, give them one of your mini-trency this instant!" ordered Oilan, as he hung up the call.

Bono quickly, but carefully kept his Danglo and Nutt in his Glustra at the corner of the room and took another mini-trency from it. He kept the Light Ball, which was the source of light, into a drawer beneath and left his home, latching up the door properly.

He sat on Eudolt and pulled its rein tightly so it stood up and flew through the atmosphere. Bono had activated his Ording-pendant, which provided him with oxygen in the outer space. And as for Eudolt, he had had a dose of oxygen pills, which could provide it with a gas that can substitute oxygen for five hours.

Oilan was going to sleep peacefully then, as he had remembered what he had forgotten, when his trency's notification ring beeped. It was the message from Ingers that asked to pick them up from there. Oilan was a little confused, but he didn't hesitate and texted back,

"Sorry Ingers, but Bono isn't here. He is gone to Friniwock to give Ponick a mini-trency because I forgot to give them one. Don't worry, I'll text him so he'll directly reach Meurin from Friniwock."

CHAPTER NINE

THE SECOND DROP

In Friniwock, Tivit was surprised by the soldier's words. He ordered the soldier, "Bring him here right now." The soldier, on his king's command, rushed to the gate and called the saint inside the control room.

The saint was wearing a white robe, with black collar. He had also worn a religious necklace with special beads. His nostrils were fused into one, which meant he was a Rynsil for sure.

He also held a holy stick called Norva, which had a religious symbol on its top. It also produced calm sounds when shaken. With the other hand, he had maintained a gesture, in which, he locked the thumb with his index finger and tried to keep the rest of the fingers stuck with each other.

The saint said, "I'm Manvil. I know where the second drop in Friniwock lies." "Where does it?" asked Ponick, curiously. "That region is unnamed. But I surely know where it is." replied Manvil.

"But why should we believe you?" asked Mridul, suspiciously. "You can take me chained hands and can sentence me to death if you don't find it." replied the saint, confidently.

"But what do you want in return?" asked Arjun. "Nothing." replied the saint. "That's fine." said Tivit, "I shall now order two Swan Carriages."

Saying so, Tivit made some clicks and swipes on his trency and soon after, two Swan Carriages appeared outside the Krate Palace. Manvil, Tivit, Ponick, Arjun and Mridul went outside the Krate Palace and saw two Swan Carriages. In one, sat Tivit and the saint. And in the other, sat Ponick, Arjun and Mridul.

Those Swan Carriages, that Tivit ordered, weren't automated, that is they didn't asked for location. Instead, the passengers could control it themselves.

Tivit was going to fly his Swan Carriage, on which he sat with Manvil, when came Bono on Eudolt.

Bono saw Ponick, Arjun and Mridul sitting on the Swan Carriage. Without wasting another moment, Bono rushed Eudolt and landed it outside the Krate Palace. Ponick, Arjun and Mridul saw him and were pretty confused. They came down from the Swan Carriage on which they had just sat.

Eudolt sat on his only pair of limbs and Bono descended him. He went forward and grabbed the unused mini-trency from his pocket he brought. He handed it to Ponick and said, "How can you forget it? I had to come all the way from Dema to Friniwock. Text me with this when you're done with your mission. I'll come pick you up that instant."

Ponick was slightly embarrassed. But he didn't mind and kept the mini-trency in his pocket.

Bono then ascended Eudolt and was just going to fly, when his trency's notification ring beeped. It was a message from Oilan that read,

"Bono, don't come in Dema right now. First, go to Meurin and pick Ingers, Aanya and Vicky from Meurin and then drop them at Friniwock to Arjun, Mridul and Ponick"

Bono read it and changed his decision. He decided to go to Meurin instead of Dema, to pick Ingers, Mridul and Aanya. He then held Eudolt's rein and shook it gently. Eudolt stood up and flew towards the outer space from Friniwock.

Ponick was grateful to Bono from inside. He didn't waste a second and sat back on the Swan Carriage with Arjun and Mridul. Tivit and Ponick flew the Carriages.

Manvil, the saint, was guiding Tivit and Tivit was controlling the Swan. The Swan was much easy to control. There was a joystick that controlled the direction of the Swan and a pair of 'up and down' buttons that controlled the altitude level. It also had a speed controlling regulator, which could brake the Swan in mid-air on pressing, and a screen that showed basic information like the altitude, the speed and much more. Apart from these functions, it also had a lever that functioned as a power button and a hand brake.

Ponick was controlling the Swan Carriage, on which he was sitting with Arjun and Mridul. He just had to keep up with the speed and follow Tivit's Swan Carriage.

The saint had rested his Norva on an elevated platform at the end of the carriage that served as a back support. The Norva was indeed important for the saint, but the way it was kept, wasn't safe.

It was taking quite a while on the journey, and Tivit was growing impatient. So, he increased the speed of his Carriage by rotating the speed controlling regulator towards right. In the process, the speed increased suddenly and the Norva that was kept at the back, fell down inside the dense canopy of yellow and red trees. It remained unnoticed by the saint and Tivit.

On the Swan Carriage that followed theirs, Ponick was paying attention to the direction of Tivit's carriage, so only Mridul and Arjun noticed it falling down.

"Ponick, that saint's stick fell down in the forest." said Arjun. "You mean Norva!" replied Ponick, as he suddenly applied brakes by pressing the speed controlling regulator. "Yeah, whatever that thing was, that the saint carried with him all the time." replied Arjun, who, along with Mridul, got a jerk through sudden braking. Fortunately, the two of them didn't crash their heads ahead because of the seatbelt they had worn. The carriage remained floating in the air.

"We shall find it, at any cost." said Ponick, "Manvil is a holy saint and to him, Norva is the most important. Do you have a rough estimate where it might have fallen?" "I do!" replied Mridul.

Soon, Ponick landed the carriage in the forest. Mridul was very precise. Only a foot ahead, lied the saint's Norva. Arjun went down the carriage and brought back with him the Norva. Ponick quickly rose the carriage up, after Arjun had seated back. Hopefully, to them, Tivit's carriage wasn't out of sight.

Ponick sped up and caught up with Tivit's carriage. He said, "Tivit, this saint's Norva had fallen down in the forest. But we got it before anything could happen."

Hearing this, Manvil was shocked. Had he lost his Norva, it would be considered a bad omen. Since Tivit was driving, Manvil took his Norva gratefully and from then on, kept it in his hands, safely.

For the next few minutes, the five of them flew in the air, until finally, Manvil told Tivit to land. The place where they landed, was barren, with only a few trees around. The land was all rock with traces of maroon sand.

There was an elevated piece of ground ahead of them, like a small hill. And on the top of it, there was a hollow cube made up of glass. Inside, it contained a Lin bubble that protected a vial, which contained Lunerk.

Manvil opened the gates of the Swan Carriage and stepped out, followed by Tivit, Ponick, Arjun and Mridul. The five of them stepped closer to it, when all of a sudden, the glass cube cracked.

It was the Lunerk-Hunter behind the cube, who had broken the glass cube with a stone. He had dressed the same. But, his left leg wasn't tied with a cloth, but looked normal, just like his right leg.

CHAPTER TEN

LIN BUBBLES

Ingers, Aanya and Vicky were sitting in disappointment, when Ingers's mini-trency beeped. It was the message from Oilan that told him that Bono couldn't come to pick them up. They were flabbergasted.

Ingers still had some enimons left. So, he decided to visit the market with Vicky and Aanya. He ordered a Swan Carriage with his mini-trency.

Soon enough, they were in the most famous market of Meurin, Ramove Lamen. Lamen, in Nenilan, meant market and the name Ramove was derived from the largest ocean in Meurin.

As they stepped into the market, the vibes were changed. There were many kinds of creatures, mostly among whom were two-legged. There came an aroma of the delicious Feren Tea. There were several shops of clothes, some especially for Kallan. There were furniture workshops and shops selling various types of trencies.

Amongst, it was one shop that provided a special liquid, a dish and a bangle like circular instrument. There was a table where children stood around. They had poured some amount of that special potion into the dish and dipped the bangle in it.

When they drew out the bangle, they had a film of soap inside. They blew into it to form bubbles and placed the letters they had brought into them. Unexpectedly, the bubbles didn't burst but simply flew up in the sky gradually.

Seeing this, Aanya asked about it. Ingers told her, "These are Lin Bubbles. It is a habit of children to write their feelings whenever their mood is off. But to ensure that they do not reopen it to read and experience the bad past again, they keep them in these Lin Bubbles, which cannot be destroyed easily. And so, they are unable to access it."

The three of them had deactivated their suits, but their belt was still visible. One Lin Bubble didn't go up, instead came down and struck Ingers belt.

Unexpectedly, there was a large pop sound that gained the attention of the crowd. As the bubble struck Ingers's Ording-belt, it cracked and popped, and the letter fell down.

The crowd was shocked. It only meant that Ingers had the Enzimine Potion in his belt, which was the rarest of all.

There was someone in the crowd who shouted, "What is it you're watching? He might be the so-called Lunerk Hunter. He has the Ivonick Sword in his belt that popped the Lin Bubble. Chase him!"

Ingers ran for his life, with the huge crowd of Ramove Lamen. Aanya too ran with him. But Mridul was cleverer than her. He pretended that he was not with Ingers and remained standing.

But Mridul had do something. He noticed that the shopkeepers had left their shops open. And that street of Ramove Lamen was almost deserted. Mridul went inside a shop and stole some No Sense Balls, that worthed much in Meurin.

The smoke that these balls expel when popped, makes everyone blind, deaf; they cannot smell, taste or even feel. From a shop, he even stole a protective suit, which he wore on.

He activated his Ording Belt and leaping from house to house, reached the chase. It was difficult for him to leap on houses with hemispherical roofs, but still he made it.

He popped the NSB, which stole the senses of everyone and unfortunately, of Ingers's and Aanya's as well. Mridul went forward and dragged Ingers and Aanya out, who tried hard to escape. They thought that by using the NSB on them, the crowd had gained control over them, but they didn't know they were in safe hands.

Mridul hid Ingers and Aanya in a thin lane, and also hid his protective suit after deactivating his Ording-belt. After a few minutes, when everyone gained their senses back, Mridul became a part of the crowd and misled them, saying, "I saw him; he went there with that little girl." He too started running with the crowd, but soon disappeared without having anyone noticing him.

He went back to the same lane and with Ingers and Aanya, flew on the Swan Carriage to the same deserted place where they had first landed on Meurin, waiting for Bono.

"That was a clever move, indeed," said Ingers, "And we have the real Ivonick Sword, is proved by the Lin Bubble." "But the point is that none suggested we could even do this as well." replied Aanya. "That's fine! At least now we can go back succeeded!"

And just later, Bono came on Eudolt to drop Ingers, Mridul and Aanya to Friniwock.

63

CHAPTER ELEVEN

AN ORD BATTLE

At Friniwock, all the five were shocked when the glass cover of Lunerk cracked. It fell apart and the Lin Bubble, which contained the vial of Lunerk, was held by the Lunerk Hunter! Yes, it was him. The only difference in his appearance before and then was that he had unwrapped the twisted cloth on his left leg then, which made his legs look symmetric.

It wasn't quite long when the 'Lunerk Hunter' noticed them. He considered he was in danger, and so, he grabbed the Lin Bubble and started to run away.

Had the five come a few a seconds later, they could see how he managed to open the Lin Bubble. But then he ran with the Lin Bubble itself and the chase had begun. The Lunerk Hunter had an Ording Pendant, with which he took leaps and ran.

The four too took leaps and chased him, while Manvil stood there and watched. Though they were four, they still couldn't help themselves to catch him since the location was barren and Lunerk Hunter could run farther from them.

While running, Ponick said, "We should have had the Ivonick Sword. If we had it, we could surely catch him in a matter of seconds." "We don't even know if we do have the real Ivonick Sword or not. It might be with him." "It is not with him," said Mridul, "If he had it, why would he run away like that?"

The Lunerk Hunter heard their conversation, and stopped. He took out a sword from a scabbard attached to the back of his suit and faced them fearlessly.

The four were wonderstruck. Arjun made a fire ball from his Linol and threw it at the Lunerk Hunter. He quickly managed to emerge a shield from his forearm and defend it.

Mridul stepped on the ground using an Ord and cracked the ground under his foe. The Lunerk Hunter jumped and defended that too. He then clapped his hands tight from which a force wave emerged that felled all the four.

Quickly rising, Tivit used an Ord and lifted most of the ground around them and threw them at the Lunerk Hunter at once. There was slight possibility that Lunerk Hunter was dead. Arjun then set fire on the mound. Then they just had to wait for the fire to extinguish, so that they could find the Lin Bubble that contained the vial of Lunerk.

All of a sudden, the Lunerk Hunter jumped out of the burning rocks. The four were shocked at his mighty strength. Ponick knew it and so said, "He has drunk the first drop of Lunerk; there's nothing we can do to harm him without the Ivonick Sword. We should focus on how to snatch that Lin Bubble from him."

Tivit quickly managed to dig up an underground tunnel using an Ord. All the rock that was removed was thrown at their foe, who overcame it easily. Arjun shot rows of fire balls at him. But he defended it all.

By the time, through the tunnel constructed, Ponick and Mridul reached behind the Lunerk Hunter. He started throwing waves of air that pushed Arjun back.

From the back, Mridul went forward to snatch the Lin Bubble from his pocket, when the Lunerk Hunter turned back to perform an Ord. He noticed Mridul and stopped.

Taking a large leap over their head, the Lunerk Hunter escaped from them. He didn't then waste his time and rushed forward to the Swan Carriage, which had arrived just then. Mridul caught hold of him from his waist.

A chit of paper was coming out of his pocket. Mridul guessed it was the map! He tried to take it out but Lunerk Hunter sensed it and grabbed the map.

Consequently, the map was torn and the minor part of it was in Mridul's hand. Lunerk Hunter ran, not caring for the piece of map, and sat on the Swan Carriage that awaited for him. It flew and so the Lunerk Hunter escaped.

Mridul opened it and his excitement knew no bounds when he found out that the piece of map he had with it, led to the third drop. He ran to Manvil in thrill. Arjun, Tivit as well as Ponick assembled there.

"What is it in your hand?" asked Ponick. Mridul unfolded the piece of map and showed it, "I managed to snatch it from him and be it luck or not, it leads us to the third drop!"

It read that the third drop laid in Dema and in the address section, it was mentioned the throne of the Prime Head in Richentery Palace! Their task was reduced to a mustard seed.

But they wondered, "Hadn't Oilan checked in it thoroughly when he looked for the map?" Mridul kept the chit in his pocket.

They flew back to the Krate Place on the Swan Carriage and found Bono already waiting for them on Eudolt, along with Ingers, Vicky, and Aanya as well. The four of them descended Eudolt and came forward.

Ingers questioned, "Have you found the second drop of Lunerk?" "Yeah," replied Tivit, "But the Lunerk Hunter was able to snatch it off from us."

Both the teams interchanged their stories regarding their mission, and Ingers was told their urge to return to Dema. Ponick sighed on hearing the good news that they had the real Ivonick Sword and not a fake one; and even how they were able to do it.

But then occurred a problem. Eudolt could carry only three people excluding Bono. But there were six of them.

CHAPTER TWELVE

BACK TO DEMA

Oilan was working on his trency. He received a message from the head of Transport Community of Meurin which read that his assistant had checked and approved the newly built Intergalactic Ship Station in Dema.

He didn't really want to speed up the work because the later the Saviours of Dema return to Earth, the more chance they had to secure the drops of Lunerk; but he did speed it up for their sake. Having it built, he made some swipes and clicks on the trency and messaged Bono,

"Dear Bono, I have a really good news for the four. The Intergalactic Ship Station has been completed, after I had sped up the work. They can now return back to the Earth, after helping us this much.

Soon the message was received and Bono showed it to everybody. It meant that now only Bono had to fly

Eudolt back to Dema; the rest can fly in the Enimixian Intergalactic Ship. Tivit booked tickets for them.

Soon, they travelled in the Enimixian Intergalactic Ship once more to return to Dema, much before Bono on Eudolt. They admired the newly built station on landing, which still had some finishing required.

They flew to the Richentery Palace on a Swan Carriage. At the entrance of the Palace stood Nodu, waiting for the four to come so that he could lead them to their room.

The four reached their room and drew a breath. It was almost certain that the four would quit their mission and return to Earth, when Mridul spoke up, "Don't you think, guys, that if we have come up so far, we shouldn't quit?" "You're quite excited to go further; and so I am." replied Arjun. "But what will we tell our moms?" said Aanya, as she stood worried.

"I believe that we shall stay. Because even if we go now, we'll have to have a made-up story. And you all know very well, this adventure isn't risky at all."

Everyone agreed on Mridul's point, and hence they, led by Nodu, went to Ponick's room though he was not found there. Upon further inspection, it was found that he was in the Main Court, with Ingers and Oilan and other ministers.

They seemed worried and the reason was that the third drop of Lunerk couldn't be found in the secret chest in the throne.

They sat there mulling over what to do, when quite unexpectedly Bono appeared with Manvil, with whom Oilan was not familiar.

"Sir," said Bono, "This sage requested me to take him along with me, because he would be of help to us. So, with Sir Tivit's permission, I brought him here from Friniwock."

"What's it you could help us with, the holy one?" asked Oilan. The saint replied, "I believe that Lox Riff might've hidden the third drop of Lunerk in Rasenta, because then he used to go for a walk with his child there, and had memories associated with it."

"Did he have a child?" exclaimed Oilan, who assumed he didn't. "Yeah, he did have one. But he left the world of pleasures quite early and went off to a cave to lead an ascetic life. It would be as better as soon to leave for Rasenta."

"Wait," interrupted Aanya, "We don't have enough time to go to another planet just for a drop and even when we are not a hundred percent sure if it's there or not." "Rasenta is not a planet, Aanya" replied Ponick, "It's a place in Dema itself; half an hour from here." "Oh, sorry." replied she.

The four and Ponick took their Ording-ornaments and the Ivonick Sword and along with Manvil, they waited for the Swan Carriage outside the Richentery Palace. Soon it came over and all the six people sat in it before it took off for Rasenta.

CHAPTER THIRTEEN

TO RASENTA

The Swan Carriage hovered in the air with six people. It didn't have a lack of capacity. As Aanya watched the ground below form the Swan Carriage, she felt something that touched her leg. She looked around her leg but found nothing.

Ponick, on seeing her examining the floor, asked, "What's it you're looking for?" "Nothing. I thought something touched my leg." replied Aanya. "It might be my leg; I also felt that I touched something." replied Arjun.

As it reached Rasenta after a few minutes, it landed on a rock-hard ground which was quite isolated. All that it had within the horizon was a vast stretch of the maroon sand, and a system of caves under a plateau ahead.

But the most important was the ruins of a great castle like structure that still stood there. Most of it was bricks but it was pretty enormous.

The place where the Swan Carriage landed was one of its entrance. It had a large iron gate that was locked from an iron chain and a large brick wall around it served as the boundary.

"You wait here," said Manvil, "I'll be right back within minutes." And he set off towards the cave system beneath the plateau. No one could object him, and had to wait there till he returned.

Ponick said, "This plateau is a vast one and is called Raseno. It bears a great importance in Dema. These ruins on this side were and are still called Rasenta, deriving the name from the plateau nearby.

This used to be a place of joy, where people from all age groups as well as species could find something or the other intriguing to them. Be it gaming-trencies for children, gyms or labs for the adults or elongated paths for the older people to walk in the evening. The ticket price was also reasonable.

But unfortunately it was struck with a tremendous tornado in the year 3489. It was closed then. Oilan made efforts to reconstruct it which was estimated to take eight years. But soon the elections were held two years later and then came the Jaff-rule and the Slavery Policy, and so the project was closed. Now, it is just *the remains that are left. Oilan will soon take a step to reconstruct it."*

Meanwhile, Manvil returned and they proceeded. On Ponick's say, Mridul cracked open the iron chain using his Ording-Belt. They entered and were in a large amphitheater.

It was so large that a hundred elephants could fight there at once. It had the maroon sand on the ground. There was one tall tower at one end of the amphitheatre, where the Prime Head sat to watch the show.

"Nostalgic!" mumbled the saint. "Did you just say something?" asked Vicky, at which the saint shook his head.

"It would be tough finding the third drop of Lunerk here." exclaimed Aanya. "Not if you know the exact location." replied Manvil, "If you climb a hundred steps of that Tower of the Prime Head to reach the chamber on the top, you would find an iron box that contains a vial of the third drop of Lunerk kept conserved in a Lin Bubble."

As he said these words, he started to feel dizzy. He abruptly fell to the ground and handed them a folded chit of paper. "I hope you helped my purpose of life." remarked the saint as his last words taking his last breath and with it, he vanished in the thin air as he gradually rose up.

"His soul is liberated," remarked Ponick, "Else his body would have been lying here as a corpse."

CHAPTER FOURTEEN

THE STORY OF THE SAINT

The saint was a mysterious man indeed. But his secrets no longer hid from the four and Ponick when they read the folded chit of paper that the saint had handed him. It read:

'My name isn't just Manvil; it's Manvil Riff. And I am the unknown son of Lox Riff, the one who invented Lunerk. He couldn't add any suitable mechanism on the throne to hide the map; it was just a red button behind it which if accidentally pressed, would reveal the whole secret of Lunerk.

He didn't trust it and kept in it a map, which would lead to just two drops, one in Metron, and the other in Friniwock. And for the third one, he wrote the location of the throne itself to mislead. For some reason, he told the location of the map just to Moven'C.

But it was me whom he trusted and told me the real location of the third drop along with the other two. He spent all of his life just to make the Lunerk; he couldn't risk it at all.

He secretly bore me and cut all of my social connections. I wasn't bothered at all when my father did this to me, on the contrary, I was dedicated to live for his purpose. I stayed in his home in a secret chamber. When I reached the age of twenty-one, I left my home and led an ascetic life, living all alone in a cave under the Raseno plateau, behind Rasenta.

My father asked Moven'C if he could alter the design of the Tower of the Prime Head in the amphitheater of Rasenta, and his permission was granted as he was his friend.

He altered nothing but just introduced an iron box in it that contained the third drop of Lunerk. He ejected an electric wire through the tower all the way back to my cave and connected the other end to a device with a password that only I was told.

I had entered the password in the device a few minutes before and by now, the iron box would've been opened. Though it rested quite open in the chamber, no one could ever move or open it; thanks to my father's incredible technology.

He even attached another trency in my cave. It could provide me a clear vision of the three drops of Lunerk, as well as their surroundings.

There's one more thing I want to tell you. You might be wondering that if I belonged to Dema, what I had been doing in Friniwock. Well, when I got to know that Lunerk's first drop had been stolen, I quickly rushed to Metron and told their Prime Head secretly. He informed Oilan and then you started your mission.

I then rushed to Friniwock and checked whether the second drop was secure and it was.But I knew that I couldn't stop anyone if he came for the second drop. I had sacrificed all my physical strength in meditation.

I had seen the Lunerk-Hunter and his attire through the special trency that was attached in my cave by my father and when I roamed in the city, I saw the posters stuck by you, asking people if they had seen the Lunerk-Hunter.

I reckoned you might prove helpful to me. So, I came to you and guided you for the second drop of Lunerk. But you see, I had a lot of responsibility on my head. It was just my assumption that you supported the good.

I wanted to test you once, and so, I intentionally dropped my Norva. But when Arjun, Mridul and

Ponick got it back for me, it was clear that you were pure-hearted. And so, I came to Dema again not just to get back to my cave, but to aid you with the third drop.

You have helped me so much. I just want one thing more. I want you to cover my cave with a huge boulder for good. You don't need to push it all by yourself; just remove the small rock that supports the big boulder beside it. The boulder will automatically fall down and will cover my cave.'

The four stood overwhelmed and astonished after reading this. "How could," they wondered, "a saint possess so many mysteries."

CHAPTER FIFTEEN

JAFFINOS'S PAST

The four and Ponick moved forward to the tower. Unexpectedly, they heard something hovering in the sky. When they turned, they saw another Swan Carriage landing. They found it unbelievable that the person sitting on the Swan Carriage was the Lunerk Hunter itself.

The four and Ponick activated their Ording-ornaments that instant. There was one back scabbard behind Arjun's blue suit that held the Ivonick Sword.

The Lunerk Hunter descended the Swan Carriage and it flew away back. The Lunerk Hunter had the stolen map still in his hand that was torn from one end. He slowly removed both of his accessories- the black sunglasses and the scarf on his face.

As his face was revealed, Ponick and the four were taken aback because the person whom they were calling 'Lunerk-Hunter' was none other than Jaffinos himself.

"What did you think? I will retreat from my ambition just from a limb cut out of my body." remarked Jaffinos, as he untied the piece of cloth on both of his legs. His right leg was alright, but instead of his left leg, was a mechanical one, that could be effortlessly moved.

"You must be curious. Let me tell you everything. When I ruled Dema, there occurred one incident that is the cause of all this. My ring fell down from my hand and as it touched the edge of my heel, it bounced under the throne. I bent to pick it up, when I discovered the red button.

I grew curious, and so pressed it. Suddenly, the seat of the throne cracked open, and came up a chest. In it, I found this map." said Jaffinos, showing up the map.

"It said it could lead me to the three drops of Lunerk, and it looked ancient, so, to some degree, I believed it might be true. I attached a tracker in it and always kept it with myself though I didn't take any action on it as I didn't need to.

Then when I lost from you in the battle the previous time, I lost my left leg but succeeded in escaping from you, as you all know.

I then came back to the Richentery Palace and took off with Eudolt. As I was the Prime Head, I had a lot of enimons in my trency that I managed to take away with me. I knew that keeping Eudolt with me was hectic, so I sent it back to Dema.

Using the enimons, I got a treatment of my leg, and I was provided with a permanent, but a mechanical leg. That didn't trouble me, as long as I could control it like the normal one. I also bought an Ording-ring.

One day, I came across the map in my pocket, which I had quite past forgotten. I decided to find them all; and successfully found the first drop. But there was the Lin Bubble protecting it. I had a scratch on my finger which I got from one of the sharp rocks that lay beside.

When I picked up the Lin Bubble, it unexpectedly burst and the vial in it fell down. I was overjoyed. But when I tried figuring out what caused it to burst, I found that it was my blood that flowed from my finger. You see, Arjun cut my leg with the Ivonick Sword and my blood absorbed some Enzimine Potion from it; it circulated in my body all the time.

Then I moved forward for the second drop. I got it easily, but when I tried to escape from you, you tore a piece of map, that would have led me to the third drop of Lunerk, but it wasn't unfortunate for me at all.

You see, the tracker I had placed on the map was exactly where the location of the third drop was written, and that piece was the same you took and kept with yourself. So, I easily tracked you down and came here on Rasenta."

Mridul became regretful. It was him who kept the piece of map in his pocket and brought it there all the way, along with the tracker.

"What turned you bald?" asked Mridul, to change the topic. "It was when my Head-Gem broke, its radiations turned my hairs weak and they fell off by time."

CHAPTER SIXTEEN

THE FRIEND'S ASSIST

"You won't be successful." said Aanya, "You don't know the exact location that Manvil told us before you came." "I do," replied Jaffinos, "I was told that they lie in the Tower of the Prime Head." "Who told you so?" "They did!" remarked Jaffinos.

As soon as he said these words, nine people, wearing black clothes and sunglasses, appeared on the boundary of the arena from hiding and pointed guns towards Ponick and the four.

"They, once, used to be my ministers and are loyal till date. They desire the Jaff-rule and possess Ording-bracelets."

"But they were twelve." replied Aanya. "Once, they were twelve." said Jaffinos, "But one was killed by Ponick and Mevan was killed by Mridul. Another died

in the same war. Now let me instruct you, as you are seized by me. Don't try to act smart. Just stand there, till I return after gulping the third drop of Lunerk."

The four were compelled to obey his orders. Jaffinos was standing at a distance, so it was difficult to hit him in any way. If anyone used an Ord against Jaffinos, the armed ministers of Jaffinos would shoot.

Jaffinos went towards the tower whistling, not fearing anything. He broke the gate and entered the bottom of the tower. There was a switch-board. Jaffinos pressed the button and several light-balls emerged out from the wall, thus lighting up the place. There was a spiral staircase that led to the chamber on the top. The railings and the steps, both were dusty.

Jaffinos started ascending it. With each step Jaffinos took to reach the chamber, the four and Ponick grew more anxious. Soon, Jaffinos reached the chamber. The glass of the windows were dusty and the ceiling had spider webs. There was a table made of wood, two chairs and beside it, rested the iron box.

He opened it and found the Lin Bubble. He peeled off the naturally formed coating on his wound on the finger, and blood started flowing again. He deposited his blood on the Lin Bubble and as expected, it burst. The vial fell loose in the box. Jaffinos picked it up and cleaning dust from one side of the glass of the windowpane, he waved the vial to the four and Ponick.

"They don't have any options left." thought Jaffinos, "I shall go down and in front of them, I shall consume it, after which very soon, I'll become invincible."

He descended the tower from the same dusty staircase and came in front of them arrogantly. "So you consumed it?" asked Ponick, afraid. "Not yet." he replied, "Thought you ought to see your hard work spoiled by me, the future Ruler of the Universe."

He opened his fist and showed them the vial that contained the third drop of Lunerk, which was transparent. He unsealed it, and opened his mouth wide.

Just as he was to pour it all in his mouth, something made him flick his hand; the vial dropped from his hands and the Lunerk, which had a slimy structure, was spilled on the maroon sand! "Jualin!" cried Ponick, as he noticed it on Jaffinos's foot.

It was none other than Jualin- their very own friend! It was a boa that helped Ponick live safely underground during the Jaff-rule. He used to inject his fangs on the soldiers who came nearby. He had bit Jaffinos on his foot.

Jaffinos picked up the vial and regained the Lunerk back in it. Furious, he ordered his ministers to shoot down Ponick. But they did nothing.

Now more furious, he shot an Ord on one of his ministers. The minister's sunglasses were tossed off from the effect of the Ord. Jaffinos, Ponick and the four stood astonished, as they realized that the minister's eyes was closed; he had fainted!

Jaffinos, who felt a bit worried, shot eight more Ords towards the ministers, which tossed off all of their sunglasses. Each one of them had fainted, but still had the guns in their grip. It was at this moment, Jaffinos knew he messed up.

He quickly went for the vial and was about to drink it, but Arjun had reacted faster. He had created a small tornado from his Linol that sucked the vial from his hand.

Arjun handed the vial to Ponick and pulled off the Ivonick Sword from his scabbard at the back. Jaffinos ran for his life. Arjun chased him with the legendary sword. Jaffinos's swan carriage had arrived by the time.

"Aim for the pendant!" ordered Ponick, who was standing behind. Arjun obeyed him and instead of his body, he struck the Ivonick Sword on his Ording-pendant. The jewel of the pendant broke and from it, fell three things- two immiscible drops of Lunerk that had different shades and the Divone.

Jaffinos didn't care for them, but for his very own life; he rushed to board the carriage. Arjun stopped at the incredible sight of Divone that looked like a black pearl. This provided Jaffinos just the surplus time he needed to elude from the four. He boarded the Swan Carriage and pressed the swift mode option. He flew back to his confidential bastion, with a normal, broken-pendant hung on his neck; he could not use it as it didn't had the Divone anymore.

Jaffinos had escaped and the four stood there. Arjun bent down and wondered at the three components that had laid in Jaffinos's pendant. Ponick and the three approached and had a view of it. "This black pearl is the Divone that is soon going to die." said Ponick. "Why so?" asked Vicky. "Because it is not enclosed in an ornament. Just like a fish dies without water, it also dies when not present in an ornament."

"And these slimy drops must be Lunerk." guessed Arjun. "Absolutely." said Ponick, as he regained them

in the same vial as the third drop of Lunerk was. "This small vial contains an extraordinary potion- the three drops of Lunerk at once. One must just swallow it to become invincible. It shall be kept safe."

Just then, Jualin slithered on the maroon sand and approached them. "You saved us today, my friend!" whispered Ponick in the language of the snake. The snake too hissed something for a few minutes. It then climbed Arjun's head and hissed again.

"It told me that from a bush in Dema, it watched our tensed faces, but couldn't guess our problem.It managed to conceal in the Swan Carriage and came here to Rasenta. It went under the sand when it found nothing serious. But when Jaffinos again approached and the men came out from cover, it knew they were foes.

It advanced to each of the nine ministers and bit them to death. Then from under the sand, it went to Jaffinos and bit him too. It said that we took so much time in finding the drops of Lunerk because we were missing a part of us, who was Jualin itself. It also said that it liked to slither on Arjun's hairs." The four of them and Ponick guffawed at this.

"But why Jaffinos was not killed by Jualin's venom?" asked Vicky, curiously. "He had two drops of Lunerk within him." replied Ponick.

Soon, the Swan Carriage arrived for them. When travelling from the carriage, Arjun asked Ponick, "Why did you tell me to aim for the pendant?"

"Because even if you had struck his body, he had a fair chance to escape. But now, though he has escaped, we have recovered the Lunerk. Now I have a task for Aanya." "What's it you want me to do?" asked Aanya.

"You see that cave below. That is Manvil's. You know the rest." Aanya remembered Manvil's letter and struck lightening from her belt to destroy the small rock beside.

As told by Manvil, the big boulder beside, with no support anymore, automatically rolled down and covered the cave.

A Tricky Venture

The carriage was proceeding to the Richentery Palace, when they heard some cries of an animal. It was another dragon like creature that looked like Eudolt and didn't had tail and the front claws.

But it was not Eudolt; their color didn't match. It was flying just beneath the carriage.

"It's an Eligon! Eligon is the same species to which Eudolt belongs. I guess Arjun broke its eggs when it left his tornado. The tornado was attracted towards the eggs and broke them. Now it is furious." Ponick pressed the swift mode option.

"So what do we do to escape?" asked Arjun. "We cannot kill it; Eligons are near to extinction. Our future generations would see just fossils if kill this one. We need to go and land on his face and block its nostrils. Without oxygen, he will go dizzy and eventually discontinue the chase." "That's something

tough!" replied Vicky. "But Aanya would do it easily, won't she?" said Mridul. "Of course not!" replied she.

"Jokes apart guys, but tell me what we can do." exclaimed Ponick. "I have an idea!" yelled Vicky, "What if we simply go to the Richentery Palace? We'll call Eudolt and have them fight with one another. That would be entertaining as well."

"Absolutely not!" replied Ponick. "This Eligon is a wild one but our Eudolt in tamed. Moreover, this Eligon is heavier and stronger than our Eudolt. It may not look like but believe me, it's a Juttin. Eudolt definitely doesn't stand a chance against him." "So how do we stand one?" exclaimed Arjun. "You demolished the Jaff-rule, prevented Jaffinos from getting the Lunerk. You have capabilities, Arjun. I assure you can."

"Can't he make a tornado and defeat it?" asked Aanya. "That's a riskier option." "Why?" "Because now, Arjun's specialty is Fire. He can make tornadoes, but not that big that would compel it to let us go. He'll get more furious if he gets hit with a tornado that can't even harm him."

"So we have no options left." sighed Arjun. "Yep, but only to go and block his nostrils." "How does he get so weird ideas?" whispered Vicky to Mridul.

Arjun, fearing a bit, jumped down on his body. It was scaly and dusty, as if it hadn't bathed for weeks, and definitely it hadn't.

As he jumped down, unfortunately, the Ivonick Sword fell from its scabbard. But fortunately, Arjun reacted quickly and used his Linol to prevent the sword from falling down.

"Please lower the carriage, do what I say." said Arjun. Ponick obeyed him and lowered the carriage. Arjun then handed the Ivonick Sword to Aanya, who sat at the corner. It was wise; he didn't need the Ivonick Sword and it was inconvenient to carry.

Arjun crept forward towards its face. The Eligon didn't feel anything. First, its scaly skin got no senses, and second was that he was too heavy already, that Arjun's weight was negligible.

The Eligon's horns were at the right distance. Arjun wrapped each of his arms on his horns and got a good grip. With his foot, he tried to cover his nostrils. The creature bent his head in order to fell Arjun off. But Arjun had a good grip. Moreover, it became easier for him to cover his nostrils. The creature felt a lack of oxygen and opened its mouth.

"Jump in his mouth Arjun!" yelled Ponick, "Tickle his tongue!" "Are you mad?" said Mridul. "Have trust in

me. I tell you."

Arjun heard Ponick and left the grip of his horns. As he fell downwards, he clung his nostrils and swung right into his mouth. He moved his fingers and toes on his tongue to tickle it. He had caught hold of his tooth to prevent it from swallowing him.

To everyone's surprise, the Eligon unexpectedly vanished into thin air, and Arjun was dropped in the jungle. But Ponick, very skillfully, moved the Swan Carriage towards Arjun and Mridul caught hold of his hand.

Vicky gave Mridul a hand to pull Arjun up onto the carriage, when he noticed three awkwardly grown flat moles back on his neck. Ignoring their disgust, Vicky helped Mridul and they together pulled Arjun up back into the Swan Carriage.

"What was that?" asked Aanya, wondering. Ponick chuckled at this. "Don't offend!" said he, "This was all just a prank!" "Seriously?" gasped Arjun. "Yes, it was a part of Professor Ingers's experiment. That Eligon was a fake one. It didn't exist at all. But still it was able to trick you."

Arjun said, "So you lied to us all the time- about my tornado breaking its eggs, and it was near to extinction; jumping into his mouth and tickling his tongue would make him faint, and that I cannot defeat an Eligon with the tornadoes I can still make."

"One needs to lie multiple times to execute a single prank, isn't it?" replied Ponick, hoping that the four don't get furious to him.

Soon, they reached the Richentery Palace and after returning their Ording-ornaments, they went for the newly built Intergalactic Ship Station. Oilan had already booked the tickets for them and had handed them over.

Through the V.I.P. corridor, they boarded the ship and waved goodbye to all those who had come for their departure- Toff, Nodu, Ponick, Ingers and Oilan.

"We'll miss you all!" cried Aanya, as the Enimixian Intergalactic Ship flew back to the Earth.

CHAPTER EIGHTEEN

THE GOOD NEWS

The ship landed in the same dense forest on the Earth from where the four boarded it. After having the four left, the ship flew back into the sky. It was peak afternoon in the forest.

The four drank the Transporting Solution, provided by Ponick, and thought of their rooms. As expected, they were teleported to the desired destination. It was three in the afternoon.

Luckily, both of their mothers were having an afternoon nap. Thinking what to lie, Arjun and Vicky entered their room.

"Should we tell her again that it was just a dream and that she could have a check-up from a physician." suggested Vicky. "Of course not; it was just a blind luck that she believed. Not this time we can play it again. She will definitely know."

Having this idea rejected, they sat down to think. Suddenly, their door opened and Mrs. Verma entered. The four missed a heartbeat. "You seem fresh. Didn't you have a nap?" asked Mrs. Verma as if nothing happened.

They couldn't understand. There were two possibilities- whether their absence went unnoticed or their mother was playing a game.

"No, we didn't." replied Vicky, stammering a bit. Arjun continued, "We were making plans for the vacation." "Very well," replied their mother, "Will you please water the plants now; they are beginning to parch." "Sure." they replied.

They then headed towards the small kitchen-garden in their home. Vicky began to fill the mug, when Arjun noticed a rolled piece of paper half dug in the soil of a plant. He took it out and unrolled it. It had text that had been printed from a computer and delivered a message from Ponick. It read-

'When you helped us so much, can't we help you too? We had placed a clone of you all the time when you hadn't been here. You need not tell your mom a made-up story. Your absence went unnoticed. The clone run everything smoothly. It was created by Ingers's machine- same that created the fake Eligon. Hope you adore my gift.'

The two of them were wonderstruck. They need not worry anymore. Excitedly, after watering the plants, they called Mridul and Aanya. They too had found the same letter! The four were overjoyed.

Two days later, Mrs. Verma received a call. It was from Mrs. Upadhyay, Aanya and Mridul's mother. Her husband had been in coma for past six years.

"My husband," said she, weeping. Vicky's mother impatiently asked, "What happened to your husband?" "He..." stammered Mrs. Upadhyay, "He is back from coma." Mrs. Verma had tears of delight, just as Mrs. Upadhyay had. "He will soon be discharged from the hospital."

Arjun and Vicky were standing beside their mother. They too heard the news and were delighted.

On the next day, they visited the Upadhyays. Mr. Upadhyay was still on bed rest. The three elders were in the same room, discussing. The four were in the *other room, enjoying themselves. They had no burden of exams; their school was yet to start.*